Annal
Please-L

MW01047273

Vol. 3

My OVERWHELMING Week
Carole Lyn Woodring, author
Issac Sternling, illustrator

Annabelle Merriday has 156 secrets!
She gives away some of her secrets, and discovers new
ones, in her stories. Her younger brother, Andrew, also
has adventures and tries to discover Annabelle's secrets.

Some of the secrets in <u>My OVERWHELMING Week</u>
are about what to do when:

1. you're running out of time, and everyone is too busy
   to help you!
2. someone (perhaps you) makes a big mistake!
3. you really want to be a winner, but you're afraid
   you're not good enough!
4. you, or someone else, is being teased or bullied!
5. you and your family miss someone who has gone
   to heaven!

Also available in the series:
Vol. 1 – <u>My COMPLICATED Week</u>
Vol. 2 – <u>My IMAGINARY Week</u>

Annabelle thinks you'll laugh at strange things that
grown-ups do and say, and she hopes you'll enjoy her
stories & secrets. Will you keep or share her secrets?

www.AnnabellePleaseDontTell.com

First paperback edition 2018
First e-book edition 2018

ISBN 13: 978-1986946377 (Libraries and Academic Institutions)
         10: 1986946371
ISBN 13: 978-0-9908180-2-1 (Retail Print Volume)
         10: 0990818020
E-book links at our website and Amazon.com (Kindle edition)
Links for libraries and academic institutions, as well as expanded distribution channels for booksellers and foreign sales, available at Amazon.com.

Madison, CT
Learn more about the series, and find activities, events, and resources at: www.AnnabellePleaseDontTell.com

Acknowledgments

In memory of my mother,
Helen Pauline Ferrari Woodring Gottlieb,
who graciously followed rules while creatively casting
elegance in her wake.
A true Cinderella, she left us quietly and stoically,
with her dignity and humor intact.
~Appreciation to my sources for love: dear friends and
family members who remain faithful, in good times and bad.
You truly are my wellspring for energy to move forward.
~Gratitude to my illustrator (Isaac Sternling) who is an
absolute joy in collaboration, and
my DanceSport pro (Dmitry Nikolaevich Savchenko) who
has helped me remain centered by reminding me,
"You must find yourself before each step."

This series is for children finding *themselves*,
in preparation for *their* next steps.
Each of you is beautiful in your unique way!
Remembering that fact will help you cope with
whatever seems overwhelming.

Carole

For my dad, the best of men.

With special thanks to Inok Magliaro, Bong Sternling, and,
of course, Carole, for the opportunity to collaborate on this
book.

And, of course, eternal gratitude to my partner, Jackson, for
all his love and support.

Isaac

Hidden Springs Elementary School

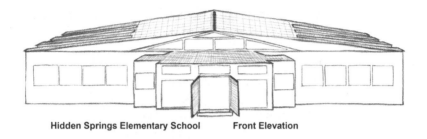

Hidden Springs Elementary School   Front Elevation

From Annabelle-Please-Don't-Tell!:

Dad explained that an "elevation" drawing

shows a wall of a building. This is an

elevation of the front of my school. You can

imagine that you have just stepped off my bus

with me: this is what you would see.

I love my school, but the idea of beginning

third grade seems a little overwhelming right

now! I'm glad that my best friend, Kayla, will

be nearby in her fourth grade classroom.

KEY
★ My classroom
1 Garden
2 Lunchroom
3 Library
4 Media room
5 Offices

This is a piece of a "floor plan" drawing.

My puppy chewed up 3/4ths of the paper! If my school had no roof, birds could look down into these rooms and halls. It would be cool if a bird came to class! I drew arrows to show where I walk from the front door.

Here are pictures of important people (and dogs) sharing this overwhelming week with me:

Table of Contents

1

--•••••--

Lucky's Unlucky Day

"Look at this exciting week!" I exclaim.

"'Overwhelming week' is more like it," says Mom, yawning at the calendar. I've learned to be patient with grown-ups, especially early in the morning.

I have secret worries about this week, but today will be great. Tomorrow will be the first day of September and the first day of third grade for me. Second grade was fun but third grade will be funner. Grandma Merriday insists that "funner" is not a real word, but it tells what I mean.

On the calendar for today is of one of my favorite words: "shopping."

"YIPPIE!" I shout.

"Yippee!" echoes my brother Andrew-I-Do-Too. He can't read, yet, but he mimics everything I say and do.

"Shopping. Ugh!" murmurs Mom. She sips from her extra large, coffee mug.

"Now, Emily," Grandma Merriday says to her, "these children need new clothes; they are growing like weeds!" Weeds? I'm not insulted because she's talking in grown-up's code. Her code words can be more confusing than "funner," in my opinion. I eat my cereal while Grandma explains several papers to

Mom.

"Emily, my dear, on this list are the school clothes and birthday party items you need to purchase. These other two lists are for supplies suggested by Annabelle and Andrew's new teachers. Just one trip to the Hidden Springs Mall should do it."

"Mall! Mall crawl!" Andrew yells. We do a silly dance step I invented with my friend Kayla. We also pretend to carry heavy bags that make us wobble. Grandma smiles; Mom frowns. Dad's away but he watches us through Mom's iPad. I hear his laughter.

"I wish you were home from your business trip, Trevor," Mom says to Dad. "You're more

patient about shopping than I could ever be."
She turns to me.

"Oh well, Annabelle, I appreciate that you agreed to share birthday celebrations with Grandpa Weinstein on Saturday. It will be fun to celebrate doubly strong! He and your Grandma Weinstein will soon be here from North Carolina. You'll be turning eight right after Grandpa turns nine times eight."

"Seventy-two!" I say. I love math.

"We'll have a fantastic party," Mom promises, "even though it will be a week before your real birthday. On your real birthday, you may choose a restaurant."

Dad speaks from the iPad, "Mom's ready

to go out to eat at the drop of a hat!" That's

another example of weird, grown-up's talk.

"May I open my gifts at this party?"

"There might not be gifts for you because

it's really an '**un**-birthday' for you: like in

Alice in Wonderland." *What? Maybe a joint*

birthday party is not a good idea! I look

closely at her face. Mom winks. Some

grown-up's jokes feel like pinches.

*****

At the mall, we check Mom's phone. Kayla and her mom, Mrs. D (Mrs. Davis's nickname), already shopped during their vacation in Atlanta. They texted photos so we could find similar outfits here in Pennsylvania. Kayla is in a grade ahead of me, but we still like to dress like twins.

I'm allowed to choose a pair of sneakers, a book bag, three tops, and three bottoms. I'll be set for three days of the school week, leaving two days for old clothes. Dad said we have to "stick to our budgets."

The girls' department is overwhelmingly

full of choices: stripes, sparkles, shooting

stars, animal prints, story characters—all I

could wish for in every color I like. "Look,

Annabelle!" exclaims Mom. "How fortunate:

a pretty, purple jumper and striped top in

your size. They match the style of Kayla's
new, yellow jumper and top." *Awesome!*

Andrew is whining that he's hungry. He's
always hungry. Racing around, we are
unable to match Kayla's other outfits, but we
find many good things I need. I'm so happy.
It's like floating in the air!

"Now for Andrew's outfits," Mom says.

"No 'fits," says Andrew firmly. "Pizza!"

"You're just like your father," says Mom.
She picks him up and gives him a kiss.

While we eat at the food court, Mom
checks the lists from our new teachers.

"I know I'll like Miss Burton," I say.

"Kayla had a great time with her last year."

"And Andrew will like his pre-school teacher," Mom predicts. "Mr. Robinson is a 'vet.' That's short for 'veteran.'"

"You 'vet,' too!" says Andrew with a mouth full of gooey, pizza cheese. Mom laughs. "A different kind. I'm a veterinarian: a doctor for animals. Mr. Robinson was a soldier."

"Soldiers!" shouts Andrew, pointing to two men in uniforms, sitting nearby. "I want soldier stuff for school!"

Luckily, in the boy's department we find camouflage pants and a green t-shirt!

Andrew does his happy dance.

"You need two more outfits," says Mom.

"No. These 'nuff," insists Andrew. That's Andrew's way of saying "enough."

"I could use your leftover money for two more outfits," I suggest. Andrew thinks.

"No, I get more soldier 'fits," he decides. Mom and I laugh.

"What happened to 'nuff fits?'" Mom asks with a wink. She looks at me. "You need to try on your old leotard before the ballet team tryouts on Saturday. This really is going to be an overwhelming week."

She is right about that, even though she doesn't know that I'm secretly nervous about the tryouts. I focus on helping her persuade Andrew to choose additional, appropriate outfits for school. We are standing in line to

pay for them when Mom's phone rings.

"Tell them I'm on my way!" Mom says in

her most serious voice. "Follow our protocol,"

she adds mysteriously, while handing

Andrew's bag to me. "I'll be there stat."

Mom says "stat" instead of "a.s.a.p." (as soon

as possible). For example, she'll say,

"Go to bed, stat!" or "Wash your hands, stat!"

Now, she takes Andrew's hand. "Children,

I must hurry to the animal clinic. Mr. and

Mrs. Rule's dog was hit by a car. I'll drop you

off at Grandma's Merriday's home. We'll

finish shopping tomorrow, after school."

"Wait! Lucky was hit? Oh no! I want to

go, too. Please take us straight to your

animal clinic to save time," I implore.

"Good idea, Annabelle!" We rush out to

our car. We must save Lucky! He is the

second sweetest dog in the world—after our

Yap-A-Doodle, of course.

*****

At the clinic, we zip into Mom's special

parking space near the back door. We run

inside. I lead Andrew to the waiting room.

Mrs. Rule is crying. Sitting beside her is a

teenager who works at our grocery store.

Andrew grips my hand so tightly it hurts.

"Where are Lucky and Mr. Rule?" I ask.

"They're with your mother's assistants,"

Mrs. Rule replies. "They asked us to wait out here. I'm sorry for crying. "I feel so…"

"Overwhelmed?"

"Exactly, Annabelle!" I pat her hand gently. Andrew pats Mrs. Rule's knee.

I wonder how Lucky got onto the road but I don't want to ask, right now.

"Mom is a very good doctor," I say. "She will help Lucky."

"Yes, thank goodness," says Mrs. Rule.

"I'm so sorry!" says the boy.

"You were driving? You hit Lucky?"

"Yes," he admits. "I passed my driver's test last week, but I did a stupid thing, today. I looked down at my phone, and that's when...." He drops his face into his hands.

"Mom fix Lucky," says Andrew.

I hope Andrew is right! So far this has been a very **un**lucky day for sweet Lucky!

2

First Day

It's exciting to walk into my new
classroom. Boys and girls are talking and
giggling. I hear a song that I remember from
the movie *"The King and I."* Aunt Leslie and
I sang the lyrics about getting to know all
about other people—getting to like them, and
about a teacher being taught by her pupils.
Students teaching the teacher? That part
seems weird. Miss Burton, my new teacher,
is at the chalkboard, and I see a boy I don't
know at a pod of desks. There are bright
colors on posters, rugs, bookshelves, and flags

that hang from the ceiling. It looks like there

was a color explosion in here: red, yellow,

blue, orange, green, purple, and even pink.

The room smells like markers, sharpened

pencils, and glue. The desks are labeled with

names—oh! there is "ANNABELLE" on a

desk for me. Daniel and Chuckie are already

standing on either side of my chair. Miss

Burton turns off the music and closes the

door.

"Students, please settle in your seats," she

says. I like that she doesn't call us

"children." I feel bigger in this classroom.

"We are going to have a great year," Miss

Burton announces. "We'll work with

multiplication, division, two-dimensional

shapes, stories from other countries, various

forms of composition, and much more." *Yikes!*

Sounds overwhelming.

"Best of all," Miss Burton continues, we'll

learn about other cultures. We will feel like

world travelers." World travelers? Cool! I

have wondered how that would feel.

 Each pod of desks has

a globe. Daniel spins

ours. Other kids notice.

Now, all the globes are

spinning. We're

laughing. Miss Burton rings a hand bell. We

become quiet. She smiles and points to a

shelf of pretend mailboxes.

"This year, you'll exchange letters with

pen pals from other countries." *Fun!* I

wonder if a student in another country will

share secrets with me. "Also," she adds, you

may write letters to your classmates here."

She clicks on a laptop. A photo of last

week's "Welcome Back to School Night"

appears on a screen behind her. I'm in the

crowd with Mom, Dad, and Andrew-I-Do-Too.

"Today, we'll learn more about each

other," Miss Burton says. "I have the fact

sheets that you filled out last week. You'll

guess who wrote each one, and then I'll

display an image of the writer." A game!

Of course, the other students guess me

right away from my facts: "Hazel eyes and

messy red hair." They laugh when she

mentions my nickname "Annabelle-Please-

Don't-Tell!" It's a name my family created

because of my 156 secrets. When Miss

Burton reads the part about my Havanese

puppy "Yap-A-Doodle," I suddenly remember

something Mom said at breakfast.

"Lucky is recovering from surgery. I'll

know more about her prognosis, tonight. She

may not be able to walk and run." I feel a

tear—*Oops*—I need to pay attention! Miss

Burton is reading another student's facts: "'I

came from Florida. My parents were born in Cuba and they speak Spanish. When I get excited or nervous, I speak Spanish, too.'"

Miss Burton adds, 'This is perfect for our studies this year." She reads on: "'I do karate. My favorite color is orange and my favorite food is fried yuca fingers.'"

"YUCKY FINGERS?" shouts Victor. "Who eats yucky fingers? I'm going to vomit!"

"Sit down and be quiet so you can hear correctly," Miss Burton demands. Victor does. She tells him, "You and I will research this food, later." She projects an image of the new boy onto the big screen, and then nods to him. "Let's welcome Carlos Flores."

"Gracias, he says shyly." I'm secretly glad he likes orange. On the bus, Victor teased me about my orange sneakers. Victor is good at art, but I don't always like his opinions.

Later, we learn about the earth's rotation. Then, we review last year's math. The lunch buzzer sounds. *Hurray!* I'm very hungry. Miss Burton asks me to walk with her so we can talk privately. *Uh oh. Did I do something wrong already?* This feels truly

overwhelming.

Miss Burton asks me a special question.

She asks me to keep this a secret until she

talks to Carlos. *Yes! I love secrets.*

The third-through-fifth-grade lunchroom has big tables and many food choices. I wish Grandma Mcrriday were here. She likes to tease that I "eat like there is no tomorrow." Of course I know there is always a tomorrow!

After lunch, Mr. Mason teaches our first "special" class: music. He points to a big, USA map while we sing about the names of the fifty states. He passes out copies of the map and a list of abbreviations. We must match the abbreviations to the correct states on our maps, tonight. *Homework tonight!*

As we line up to go out to the buses, Miss Burton explains, "Our school pairs new students with buddies. Annabelle Merriday will be buddies with Carlos Flores, who could

teach us about Cuba." Hmmm—like the

teacher learning from her pupil in *The King*

and I." Victor is making devil's horns behind

Carlos's head. Dad would say Victor needs

"an attitude adjustment." Miss Burton adds,

"And we'll learn about other countries from visitors to our class." *Wow! So much is happening. I'm in a third grade tornado!*

*****

At my bus stop, I see Grandma Merriday with Andrew-I-Do-Too and Yap-A-Doodle.

"Your mother is still at work, and your father stayed at the airport to meet your other grandparents," she explains.

"Oh no!" I say. "I need Dad to take me to buy favors for the birthday party, and my dance stuff, and..."

"Whoa, Annabelle." Grandma says.

"Whoa, Annabelle," echoes Andrew, galloping around. "Horses!"

"No time to 'whoa,'" I reply. "I'm becoming

a world traveler, a buddy, and a pen pal—

and probably more stuff I don't know about,

yet. Plus, I have *HOMEWORK!* All this

makes me hungry." Grandma sighs.

"Oh dear, we're in the same boat!" she

says. This is a weird, adult way of saying she

feels as overwhelmed as I do. She goes on,

"While I was getting ready for your other

grandparents to stay in my home, my clothes

washer leaked all over the floor. I had no

time to make after-school snacks. You may

have milk and a banana. Everyone will be

here soon. Maybe tomorrow Mom or Dad will

take you to the party and dance shops."

We hurry home. I gobble and drink fast, then run upstairs to try on my old leotard. I try every way possible but it is *totally* too small. What if the shop is out of my size? I *really* wanted to make the team! Why did I

have to  grow so

much?

3

They're Here!

I go back down to the kitchen, hoping

Grandma will help with my homework. Mom

bursts into the kitchen from the garage.

"I have something special to show you,"

she exclaims, pulling her iPad out of her tote

bag. That bag is enormous; Andrew-I-Do-Too

once hid inside it when we played hide-and-

seek. I secretly wish I would get an iPad for

my real birthday.

"Look at the screen," Mom says."

It's Lucky! Standing up! Wait...one of his

legs is wrapped with white strips and he has

a cone to prevent him from licking them.

"I had to reset bones and patch wounds,"
Mom reports, "but he will heal."

"Butt heal," says Andrew, pointing to a
bandage on Lucky's rear end. We laugh.

"Good work, Emily," says Grandma
Merriday.

"May we buy a 'get-well' toy for Lucky
when we go shopping?" I ask.

Mom gasps. *"More* shopping?"

"Please don't sound exasperated, Emily,"
Grandma Merriday advises. "You are not the
only one having an overwhelming week."

"Egg-as-per-tated?" Andrew looks
puzzled.

I think *I'm* exasperated.

"Mom, grown-ups tell us to set priorities.

It's *totally* '*high priority*—*CRITICAL*' that I

get party favors and decorations, *AND a*

leotard! Sorry for shouting."

"You egg-as-per-tated, too," Andrew

declares, with his hands on his little hips.

We're interrupted by voices behind the door

from the garage. Dad enters, grinning.

"They're here!" he announces. Behind

him, we see Grandpa and Grandma

Weinstein.

"Where are Annabelle and Andrew?"

Grandpa asks, even though he is staring

directly at us. "You, two, are too big to be my

grandchildren." He turns to Dad. "Where did you hide my grandchildren, Trevor? I think my grandchildren are gagged and tied up somewhere! Form a search party!"

"*NO! HERE! Me Andrew!*" My brother, who loves attention, stands as tall as he can.

"Well, that's a relief because I'm too tired

to search the whole house," says Grandpa.

Suddenly, everyone is hugging and kissing.

"What in the world do you feed these children

to make them grow so fast, Rose?" he asks.

"You'll find out right now, David,"

Grandma Merriday answers. "We're having

a dinner you like: roast chicken, mashed

potatoes, and beet salad."

Fortunately, Grandma made a lot. I fill

my tummy until it bulges. I have to say "No,

thank you" for strawberry pie.

"*What?*" all the adults ask in unison.

"I eat hers," Andrew offers.

I explain that it's now time for critical

shopping, but I keep the surprise party a secret from the two who don't know about it.

"Yes," Mom says quickly. "Please excuse us while we make a rapid, little trip."

*****

In the car, I repeat my question about a toy for Lucky.

"If there is enough time, we 'll take care of all of your priorities," Mom promises.

"Hurry!" We race through the party store, collecting fun things; out to the dance shop's

ballet slipper section; into the pet shop; out to the car; and down the road. It's amazing how much we can accomplish when we feel overwhelmed. Relieved, I enter the kitchen behind mom. *Wait!* We forgot something *very important. This is an emergency!*

"I need to call Kayla *STAT!*" I shout.

"Homework comes first," replies Grandma Weinstein, holding my school papers.

"I can't possibly memorize abbreviations for fifty states' names, tonight! My head is too full of other things."

"Let's start by filling in the blanks on the list," Grandma Merriday suggests.

"Then," says Grandpa Weinstein, "I'll share my secret method for memorization. You love secrets, right?" I nod.

"And, I saved your pie," says Grandma Merriday, "so you'll have enough energy. We'll be a team together."

"Ok," I say. We sit down at the table. "Is your secret method difficult, Grandpa?"

"Very simple." He reaches over and steals a piece of my pie with his fork. "Thank you, 'Bella Annabella.'" That's his way of letting me know he thinks I'm beautiful. "Most of the states use the first two letters, or the first letter plus the last letter. For the remaining states, you just make up a little story."

"A story?"

Grandpa chooses three of our colored pencils. He circles thirty-one states with green. He circles ten states with blue. He circles nine with red.

"What do you notice about the green ones?" he asks me.

"Most of those use the first two letters,

like 'AL' for Alabama. States that have two-word names (like New Hampshire) use the first letter of each word (like 'NH'). Also, I see that the blue states use the first and last letter, like 'GA' for Georgia."

"Smart girl," Grandpa says, beaming.

"Now we'll make up one-sentence stories for the red states. Alaska can't use 'AL' because Alabama took that abbreviation. Alaska uses 'AK.' What words start with 'k'?"

"Uh...kite. Kangaroo. King."

"KITE!" yells Andrew, "Want kite!"

"Ok, Andrew," says Grandpa. "We could say, 'I went to **Alaska** to fly my **kite**.' Your Your map indicates you'd have to travel very far to fly a kite in Alaska. That fact will help

you remember. Now 'AK' = Alaska."

"Magic!" I say. "Let's do the other ones!"

Dad intervenes: "Andrew's going to bed to

rest up for pre-school's first day." Andrew's

face wrinkles up. Oh no, a tantrum's coming!

4

·-·•••••·-·

No Go!

It's hard to get ready for my second school day while Andrew-I-Do-Too is screaming *"NO GO! NO-O-O. NO! NO!"* His words fly up and down our stairs, and boomerang around the rooms. I shut my door to get dressed. I guess everyone has a day when they don't want to go to school, but I can hardly wait. Andrew's behavior, this morning, seems weird because he usually wants to copy me.

Normally, Mom brushes the tangles out of my hair but now she is focused on little Mr. *NO GO!* I put on a top and pants that I think my friend Kayla will like. I can't remember

what I wanted to call her about! By the time

I get down to breakfast the house is quiet.

"Your dad and Grandpa told Andrew they

will take him on a 'special mission just for

men,'" Mom explains. "Grandma Merriday is

at her home, next door, taking care of

Grandma Weinstein who picked up a bug on

the airplane yesterday."

"Eww, was it a creepy, crawly bug?" Mom

looks perplexed; then she smiles.

"A sickness bug. A Virus."

"You mean, a 'cold,' Mom. But not as in

shivering from 'cold,' although Grandma *was*

shivering yesterday. Why are your answers

so confusing?"

"My answers? Because your questions....

oh never mind, Annabelle!" We both laugh.

*****

My second morning in third grade goes as

fast as I could say Dad's favorite tongue

twister that starts out: *How much wood*

would a woodchuck chuck if a woodchuck....

I've never seen a real woodchuck, but my

friend Chuckie and I like to recite that

rhyme. We can't do that today because Miss

Burton moved Chuckie out of my pod of

desks. Now, my new buddy, Carlos, sits near

me. He keeps his eyes down; he seems shy.

*****

At lunchtime, I walk in line with Carlos

who accidentally steps on my foot.

"I'm sorry," he says, looking down at my

new, orange sneakers.

"Do you agree with Victor that they look

ugly with my red hair?" I ask. For the first

time, Carlos stares directly at my face.

"¡No! They are very pretty. And you are

muy bonita." He blushes and looks down.

"I'm glad that I was chosen to be your buddy," I say quietly. "Is it overwhelming to be a new kid? You must have secrets about that." He looks at me with big eyes. "The kids at my old school were mean to me. Eran muy abusadores." He pauses to find a word. "Bullies." He seems very nice but still bashful. How can I help him?

"Let's talk again, during recess on the playground," I suggest. Carlos smiles.

Back in the classroom, we meet Miss Ella, a student teacher who is going to be in our classroom for the first half of the year. She has pretty, blue beads in her braids and around her neck.

We go over the abbreviations for the 50

states. Olivia and I raise our hands for every

one. "How did you two learn them so well?"

Miss Ella asks.

"I love to memorize," says Olivia. "I just

say them out loud, over and over, until the

sounds are connected in my head. Now 'C-A'

is stuck to 'California' like 'ice' to 'cream.'"

"Good work," says Miss Ella. "Is that

what you do, Annabelle?"

"No, I use my Grandpa's secret method."

Twenty-six sets of eyes stare at me: 24 sets

from the students + 2 sets from the teachers.

"Give up the secret!" demands Daniel.

I share the secret beginning with Alaska.

We have fun making up more sentences until

the lesson ends.

During recess, I run to a garden at the end

of our playground. Hearing someone running

behind me, I turn. It's Carlos. He stops and

looks down at the garden. He's still shy!

"These are nice flowers," he says. "My last

name, 'Flores,' means 'flowers' in English."

"That's cool, Carlos. My best friend's
mother owns a flower shop." He smiles.

"Did you know that Havanese dogs, like
yours, are the National Dogs of Cuba?"

"Wow. May I ask something personal?
You mentioned bad kids in your previous
school. What did they bully you about?"

Carlos looks around. Everyone is playing
games, not paying attention to us. He picks
up a stick and draws circles in the dirt. It
reminds me of when I doodle in the margins
of my homework to help myself think.

"You can trust me, Carlos. I am the best
secret-keeper in the entire town of Hidden

Springs. In fact, in the whole state of PA—

Pennsylvania. Maybe the US. Maybe..."

"But you gave up your grandpa's secret to

our entire class," he says.

"That's true," I admit, "but when Grandpa

Weinstein really wants my brother or me to

keep a secret, he makes us promise to keep it

'confidential.' Then we shake hands."

"Bueno," says Carlos. He puts out his

hand. "¿Promesa? Keep this secreto?"

"Pro-mess-a—promise! Yes, I promise not

to tell anyone until you say it's ok to share."

We shake hands.

Carlos says, "I told our class about doing

karate but not about the activity I like most."

"I think this is going to be a big secret,"

I guess. He nods.

"I was the leader in a ballet show," he

whispers.

"What a coincidence!" I exclaim. I'm going

to try out for a ballet team on Saturday. I'm

nervous; the team is already really good."

Carlos checks for anyone watching us. He

stands up and demonstrates two of the basic

ballet positions that I've tried to learn. "Wow,

that's amazing!" He turns red again.

"You are permite—I mean 'allowed' to

dance ballet because you are a girl," he says,

forgetting to whisper. We both look around.

Daniel's watching, but I don't think he heard

clearly. "When our show was on TV news,

boys called me 'sissy.' My parents were

embarrassed." He breaks his drawing stick.

"My parents said. '¡No baile!'—ballet! '¡Only

karate!'"

"Do you like karate?"

"Ok," he says quietly.

"But not as much?"

"No. Not my favorite."

"Would you like to try out with me? If we don't make the team, we can still take a class together. There were two boys in class last year." A little smile begins in the corners of his mouth...then disappears. He throws the broken stick into the garden.

"My parents mean it: '¡No!'"

"When my brother says 'No!' *my* parents say there is always a way to compromise— to make things ok."

"No comp-ro-mising for me. Mis padres dicen, *'¡*No, no, *NO!'*" Sounds familiar. I believe Carlos speaks Spanish when he is upset, but his "No" is just like Andrew's.

I nod, but I remember that Carlos's parents seemed nice at "Welcome Back to School Night" last week. I'm secretly determined to solve this problem, even though it seems overwhelmingly messy.

5

5 Positions & 1,000 Pounds!

On Wednesday, our class has fun with fractions. Then we each take a pen pal's name out of a hat. My first pen pal will be a boy in Canada. I already have lots of questions to ask him about living there. Miss Burton assigns homework: words we must be able to spell and define. By the time I get home, my head is spinning like a globe.

Grandma Merriday and Grandma Weinstein are in our kitchen surrounded by chaos—a good vocabulary word that Dad often uses to describe our major messes.

"This is the most overwhelming day of all," says Grandma Merriday.

Grandma Weinstein hands her a cup of tea and says, "It's not your fault that the cake fell. I often have that problem."

I don't see any cake on the floor. Yap-A-Doodle isn't scrunched down, looking guilty.

"Did Andrew-I-Do-Too drop it?" I ask. "Where is he?"

"No," says Grandma Merriday. "Your brother is taking a nap. The cake is right here, but it doesn't look like a cake. It rose nicely in the oven. I took it out to cool and *plunk!* Now, I feel like the cake: I rose in the morning ready to accomplish everything on my long list of tasks and now, *plunk!*"

"Grandma, you know you have made many beautiful cakes for all of us," I remind her. "I bet Grandpa Merriday loved your cakes. I also bet you miss him. I wish he were alive to made you feel better, today." She smiles.

"I'll tell you a secret, Annabelle," she says.

"One of the few things he loved more than

cake was 'Baby Annabelle.' One time I

caught him letting you have a bite of cake."

Grandma Weinstein laughs, and then she

turns to me.

"Grandma Merriday is just feeling

overwhelmed from doing too many things for

everyone," she reveals. "Look at this

fabulous fishing vest that she made

for Grandpa Weinstein!"

"That looks like a superhero's vest!" I

proclaim.

"He will feel like a superhero, when he

wears this vest on his fishing boat in North

Carolina," she replies. "Your Grandmother
Merriday included compartments for
everything Grandpa Weinstein needs when
he is out on the Atlantic Ocean. She made a
Velcro pocket for his glasses, a plastic shield
for his fishing permit, a waterproof pocket for
his wallet and phone, a zipper pocket with a
grommet to guide his fishing line when he
winds it onto a reel, a safety hook for his
pocket knife, snaps and buckles to adjust the
vest's fit—it's amazing! She even stitched his
name and phone number on it!" Grandma
Merriday looks happier now. "Try it on,
Annabelle," Grandma Weinstein offers.

It feels like an amazing costume. I stick

my finger into the grommet to feel how it will

help his fishing line move from a disk to a

reel, without tangling.

"How did you learn about all this?" I ask.

"I researched fishing vests on a computer,"

Grandma Merriday explains. "I already

knew how to sew details like buttonholes, but

I needed to learn how to use grommets and

four other things. I practiced with help from

my friend Mrs. Young." She points to a box

of fabric scraps. "Also, your Grandma

Weinstein secretly measured Grandpa

Weinstein's favorite sweater vest."

"You had to learn to do five new things?

And your friend helped you practice? You've

given me good ideas for some very difficult

things that I need to learn. Thank you."

"Are you worrying about your vocabulary

list for school?" Grandma Merriday asks.

"Even more important!"

"Well you'll figure that out, I'm sure,"

Grandma says. "However, tonight, I'll help

you with your homework." She winks.

"Ok, but may I call two of my friends

first? I need them to help me with my other

project tomorrow." Grandma agrees.

****

It seems like forever for Thursday

afternoon to arrive. Carlos and Kayla meet

me in my garage for our secret project. I'm

lucky to have my old buddy Kayla *plus* my

new buddy Carlos; now we can be friends

together. They seem happy and excited, too.

"I will be el maestro de ballet—the ballet

teacher," Carlos says, standing very tall, "if

you promise to keep this a secret."

"'Yes' to keeping it a secret," says Kayla,

"but I think you must be a grown-up to be a

real teacher or whatever you call it."

"Sorry, Kayla," says Carlos. "My parents

talk in Spanish so, sometimes, I do, too."

"Everything is ok," I say. "On our first day

in school, Miss Burton played a song from a

movie that my aunt watched with me. It was

about a student teaching a teacher from

another country—like we are learning about

other cultures this year." They look at me

like I have a duck sitting on top of my head.

"Please teach us Carlos. Kayla is on a

gymnastics team. I think she would be more interested in your karate skills."

"Cool!" says Carlos. Kayla grins, but Carlos is already investigating a pile of scrap wood that Dad stows under his workbench.

"Ok to use this?" Carlos asks, holding up a piece of an old, broken, rocking chair.

"I'm sure it would be ok. Dad used the pretty spindles from the back of that chair to make a sleeping crate for Yap-A-Doodle. Of course, Yap prefers to sleep at the bottom of my bed. Why do you need that wood?"

"Las herramientas. These are tools I can use if you want me to teach you an awesome ballet trick. Pero, primero we'll make sure you can do the five, basic positions for the tryout on Saturday. Then I'll show you secrets about this trick: a pirouette." He demonstrates it. Kayla's eyes grow big.

"I've seen pirouettes," I say, "but I feel they are definitely too overwhelming for me right now." Kayla nods in agreement.

"We'll start with first position," Carlos continues. "Numero uno is the first and it is the beginning of everything in ballet. Use first position to connect your *mind* and your *body* to work *together*. ¡*Juntos!*" I copy what Carlos does, but Kayla looks puzzled.

"I don't get it," she says. "My mind and body *always* work together—juntos."

"No," says Carlos. "Your mind is trying to figure out what Annabelle and I are doing, but your muscles need to *feel* what happens when you do this. Keep trying with us so you can bring yourself together, Kayla. No te preocupes—don't worry. You'll learn fast because you're already good at gymnastic tricks, and then I'll show you some karate tricks." Kayla gets into first position.

"Carlos, you remind me of my Aunt Leslie," I tell him. "She says mysterious things. She once told me to let her words roll around in my head until they make sense. It doesn't always happen right away, but her words eventually do make sense in a weird and wonderful way."

"I don't know about all that," Carlos says,

"but you need to turn your feet out a little

more, Annabelle. And, please pretend you

are holding a beach ball, Kayla. Both of you

stand derecho—as straight as a pencil. And

drop your shoulders." Drop our shoulders?

He demonstrates what that means.

We work and work and work! On all five

positions! Finally, Carlos says that we have

made enough progress to take a break. He

takes off his sneakers and does the most

amazing thing. He spins around in a double

pirouette on one leg. Then he spins in the

opposite direction. Yap-A-Doodle yaps and

jumps at Carlos until he stops and puts on

his sneakers.

"I can teach you, two, how to do pirouettes

using this piece of wood, under my shoe." he

offers. Kayla and I take turns trying, with

his help, until Grandma Weinstein comes

into the garage. She must have heard Yap.

"I have some milk and southern biscuits

for you," she says, "but first, I'd like to watch

you trying pirouettes."

"How do you know about them?" Kayla

asks.

"I learned when I was your age," Grandma

replies. "Annabelle's mother preferred tennis

but Annabelle inherited my dance interest."

"I can't do pirouettes, though," I admit.

"Well, Sweetie, I had a wise teacher who said that 'can't' is a dirty word. He said that the strongest men in the world can lift more than one thousand pounds: the weight of an

average, real-life horse! When those men were born, they could lift only their hands. While growing up, they practiced lifting weights. Each day they became stronger."

Sharing our biscuits and milk at the picnic table in our backyard, I smile at my friends.

"I feel that you would never tease me about things like my orange sneakers or how my hair goes wild on humid days."

"Of course not," Kayla agrees, "but, you're lucky. You can change your sneakers or tie back your hair. If I get teased for my dark skin, I can't change my own color."

"Oh no!" Carlos says. Crumbs fly out of his mouth. "In your head you know that your skin is as beautiful as your mother's, right?"

"Well...yes...I guess so. But what does that mean?"

"Bring together your happiness about

your beauty and misery about the teasing.

Mix it up. ¡Juntos! The facts of your beauty

will overcome hurt of the teasing." Kayla

looks a little cross-eyed as she does this, but

Carlos goes on, "I was bullied in my last

school for having Spanish-speaking parents

and for dancing ballet. They called me bad

names, threw dirt balls at me, dumped my

lunches onto the floor, put stinky things into

my backpack, and did even worse things—

cosas malas. So, guess what."

"What?" Kayla and I ask in unison.

"Because of my parents, I put karate

together with my problem. I worked hard at

karate skills. My mind got very busy and my body got strong. I felt brave and happy. I forgot about the kids. Then, they forgot about me. I still wish I could dance, though."

Kayla says, "I'm starting to get this juntos concept, Carlos, but you don't have to *completely* give up your ballet dreams if they are what makes you *you*." Wow, everyone is starting to sound like Aunt Leslie.

"Let's ask our parents if we can practice again before the tryouts," I suggest.

"I don't think my parents will let me come to the tryout," Carlos says, "but, if they let me come here after school tomorrow, I'll help you both with ballet and karate."

"Let's try to eventually persuade them to let you do both," Kayla suggests. "Meeting again will be our first step." We do a three-way handshake.

6

·-·•◦●◦•·-·

Help!

On Friday morning, I'm too excited to eat.

"You must eat breakfast," Dad says. "A

jet cannot take off without fuel." He and

Andrew love anything that flies. Dad likes to

made model airplanes with motors for us to

fly in our backyard. We don't put fuel into

those, of course, because they have batteries.

Right now, I feel like a helicopter whirling

out of control—or a spinning globe—or a

spiraling pencil! Just *thinking* about doing

pirouettes makes me dizzy.

*****

In class, Miss Burton says that Miss Ella

will read a special kind of story.

"This is a fable," says Miss Ella. Her voice

is soft like Grandma Merriday's. "Does

anyone know what a fable is?" she asks.

No hands go up.

My friend Olivia asks, "You mean like the

fables about foxes?"

"Yes!" says Miss Ella. "Do you remember

anything special about those stories?"

"Usually a fox tries to trick other animals

but, sometimes, he is the one who is fooled."

"Correct. Fables are short stories with

animals as characters plus a lesson—a moral.

This fable features a mouse and an alien."

"Alien!" Daniel bursts out.

"In fables," Miss Ella continues calmly,

"some of the animals are good and heroic.

Others need to learn a lesson."

"Like some people," says Carlos, looking at

Daniel. Miss Ella smiles.

"Sí—yes, Carlos. You are right. Let's see

who learns a lesson in this fable." She holds

up a book with a picture page. "Look at this

alien tangled up in a net that a hunter uses

to trap animals. Notice a curious mouse

watching cautiously from a safe distance. He

is much smaller than the helpless alien." She

reads: "The alien thrashed harder and

harder, beeped louder and louder, glowed

brighter and brighter,

and became MORE

and MORE

FRUSTRATED

and PANICKY!

Suddenly, it

sank into an exhausted heap. Its glow

dimmed."

Miss Ella uses a squeaky voice for the tiny

mouse's offer: "'I can help you, Mister.'"

Miss Ella makes beeping sounds and uses

a ghost-like voice for the alien's mocking

reply: "'Beep-It's strange-beep-I can't get -

beep-free from this trap-beep-beep! I'm from

Planet X-TRA where everyone is stronger

and smarter-beep-than mere earthlings!

How could a little-beep-squirt like *you-beep-*

help *SUPER SUPERIOR ME-BEEP-BEEP?'*

"The mouse wanted to scamper home, but

he remembered two secrets his father had

shared. Taking a deep breath, he crept

behind the alien. Carefully, he used his

sharp teeth to gnaw through the net's ropes.

Then, after running down into a deep hole, he

called back, 'You're loose. Try to remember:

1. everyone has some big abilities

2. problems are usually smaller than they

   seem.'

"The alien wiggled free from the tangles.

"'Please, Mr. or Miss Mouse,' he called out, 'Let's-beep-be friends. We could be a great pair of-beep-beep-talented explorers on your strange planet.'

"And they were." Miss Ella holds up a picture of the alien and the mouse strolling happily through the woods toward a city.

"Your assignment for next Monday is to think of an idea for a fable with animal characters and a lesson. Just write a few notes and we'll work on your stories with Miss Burton."

*****

During recess, Carlos and I rehearse the five ballet positions I want to master. Then we practice pirouettes plus karate moves that he is going to teach Kayla. Suddenly, I hear clapping. Students are watching us. Carlos looks astonished...happy...not shy!

*****

Riding home on the bus, I confide to

Kayla, "I've been worried; we forgot to buy a

new leotard and, since then, no one has had

time. I'll be embarrassed in shorts when the

other girls look *perfect* at the tryouts."

"My mom says every person is already

perfect when they are born naked," Kayla

replies. The boys behind us giggle.

"She said 'NAKED!'" one of them shouts.

"Naked, naked, naked," two others chant.

"Never mind them," I whisper to Kayla.

"Ok. I'll bring my leotard to your house,

tonight. It's red, my favorite color, so you

might think it clashes with your hair, but

it should fit you."

"Carlos has taught me not to worry about anything clashing with my hair; I'll love wearing your leotard. It might bring me good luck because you are my best, forever friend!"

Time is speeding up. I'm getting really nervous about the tryouts.

*****

On Saturday morning, it feels as though

Grandma Weinstein uses a *million* bobby pins with a red ribbon to hold my wild hair in a bun. Mom offers a lucky charm on a chain, and Carlos shows up in his karate shirt!

At the dance studio, we see ten girls and two boys warming up at the barre.

"Good luck," says Carlos, turning away. I gently grab his shirt.

"Remember the brave mouse. Please stay and help me. You can do this in your socks."

A woman at the piano strikes a loud chord.

"There are six vacancies on my team," announces Miss Marina. *Oh—156 is my lucky number!* As she calls out the five, basic positions, I do my best. When she requests unfamiliar movements, I follow the older students. Carlos and I are so excited that we do a pirouette. It works! Hurray! We try another pirrrrrr-oooou-e—*thud!* —we land in a heap on the floor! SILENCE! One giggle. Several giggles. Embarrassed, we get up.

"Miss Annabelle and her friend have tried

one method to learn dance: 'trial and error,'"

says Miss Marina. "That is better than not

trying. Now they may join my team to learn

more efficiently." *'Join'...does she mean...?*

Now, Carlos is as red as Kayla's leotard.

"Lo siento—I mean, 'I'm sorry!'" he

murmurs. "I was just helping Annabelle."

"You are talented, Master...what is your name, please?"

"Carlos. Gracias, but I...my parents...I do karate. *Only* karate."

"Well, Master Carlos, I'll explain to your parents that ballet skills help improve karate skills." *Wow, I hope that works for Carlos!*

As we leave, Mom asks Carlos and Kayla, "Are your families coming to our party, tomorrow?"

"Totally!" confirms Kayla. Carlos shrugs.

"¡Estoy en un gran problema!—I mean, 'I'm going to be in big trouble.'"

7

- • • ● ● ● • • ·

Aloha!

We return home just in time to welcome our guests who will help us celebrate the finale of our overwhelming week!

Our birthday cake looks great, after all. The sunken part is filled with whipped cream. Andrew adds raspberries and chocolate sprinkles. Dad arranges eighteen candles: 8 pink ones for my years, 7 green ones for Grandpa's 7 decades, 2 blue ones for his additional years past 70, and a yellow one for extra luck.

"Yum!" Andrew exclaims, with sprinkles

and cream all over his mouth.

"I bet you'd eat Brussel sprouts that you

hate, if we put sprinkles on them," I tell

Andrew-I-Do-Too. He giggles.

"Sprinkles on russel routs, too! Open my

gifts," he directs Grandpa Weinstein and me.

We discover that he has made a clay fish for

Grandpa and a clay star for me.

"You dancing star," he says, beaming.

Our friends and relatives offer gifts that

show they care about what Grandpa and I

love to do. Lucky watches Yap-A-Doodle

happily playing with gift-wrappings.

"What's wrong, Tiger?" Grandpa whispers.

This nickname expresses his idea that I have

the adventurous spirit of a jungle cat, plus hair that's the color of a tiger-lily flower.

"My feelings are 'falling'...like my body fell in the dance studio...like Grandma's cake fell. I'm happy that I'm dancing, but it's not fair that Lucky now walks with a limp and wears that cone on her head to prevent her from biting off her leg bandage."

"Don't worry, Tiger. It's good that Lucky and I have doctors who help us, and people who love us. I need a cane to help me walk. But, you know what? As I've become older, I've become better at doing certain things."

"What things, Grandpa?"

"Persuasion, for example. I think I did a pretty good job of persuading Carlos's parents to come to our party. How about that, Tiger?"

"You did that?" He winks. My family winks a lot. I need to practice my winking.

"It's time for me to take the floor," he says.

Code! I look at the floor as he clears his

throat. He announces to everyone, "It's a

family tradition for me to give a birthday

speech. So, I want to say that I don't know

much about ballet and karate—including

their *physical positions*. However, I have

philosophical positions about certain topics,

such as bullying." He sounds like Aunt

Leslie talking about her mysterious beliefs!

He continues, "My *first position* on bullying is

my *only* position on that topic: NO one

should bully another person, especially if he

or she has not walked in the other person's

shoes! End of speech. Thank you for this

amazing party!" So...*walk in their shoes?*

I look to see if anyone thinks Grandpa is crazy but they're clapping—even Mr. and Mrs. Flores, who speak very little English. I know Victor has never walked in my orange sneakers. If he teases me again, I'll challenge him to do a pirouette. Carlos and I can do some things that bullies cannot do.

Grandma Merriday hands me an envelope marked "8." Grandpa Merriday went to heaven when I was a baby, but he left birthday envelopes for me. Grandpa didn't know if Mom would have more babies, so he wrote on each envelope: *"For Annabelle to share with any siblings she may have."*

"I am sibling!" Andrew announces proudly.

I read the letter: *"Dear Sweet Annabelle,
You are eight! I learned how to write this
way, in cursive, when I was your age. My
handwriting is not as beautiful as your
Grandma Merriday's. It makes me laugh to
think that you might need to decipher my
cursive like a code. You are growing bigger,
so your dreams are growing bigger as well.
You no longer dream about learning how to
walk or ride a bike down the street."*

I share a secret with everyone, "I dream
about *pirouetting* down the street."

"He would say, 'Good girl,'" Dad says.

I read: *"The birds, butterflies, beetles,*

and I will be watching the wonderful things

you will do this year. Give big hugs to

everyone there for me, please.

Love, Grandpa Merriday XO!

I shake the envelope because each one

contains a keepsake plus a card with wise

words that Dad calls "Grandpa's secrets for a

happy life." A card and a photo fall onto our

rug. Naturally, Yap rushes over to sniff, but

she looks at me for permission to take them.

I snatch them up.

The photo is of Grandma Merriday when

she was young. I'm guessing she was my age.

There is a ladybug in the palm of her hand. I

give the photo to her and read the card:

"Dare: dream big, focus fully, work re...uh

...re-lent-less-ly. You'll be happier than you

can imagine."

"¡Si!" Mr. Flores claps. He nods at Carlos.

Wow, I wonder if he will let Carlos.... Dad

interrupts my thoughts, "Annabelle, I think

you inherited your love of secrets from

Grandpa Merriday. It's in your genes." I've

never found anything about secrets in my

jeans' pockets, so Dad might be wrong about

that. I send what Grandma Merriday calls a

"mental hug" to Grandpa Merriday in

heaven. Then I hug everyone else, including

Lucky and Yap-A-Doodle. Andrew-I-Do-Too

does the same, of course.

Dad says, "Let's end our party by saying 'Aloha.' Grandpa and Grandma Weinstein will be flying back to N.C. very early in the morning." Suddenly feeling overwhelmingly sad, I try to focus on what Dad is explaining. "In Hawaii, our 50th state, people say 'aloha' for both 'goodbye' and 'hello.' It signals that they are looking forward to seeing you again." Dad looks at Andrew. "'Aloha' means 'bye' and 'hi.'"

"Bye-Hi, Hi-Bye, Bye-Hi." Andrew chants.

Everyone claps. Ok, I feel better, now.

*****

After our guests are gone, Grandma Weinstein brushes out my ballet hairdo, and then kisses the top of my head.

The house is very quiet when Mom tucks

me into bed. She puts Andrew's star onto my

night table where I can see it. Then she

tacks Grandpa Merriday's card onto a board

Dad made for my wall. She doesn't react

when Yap-A-Doodle settles into her spot at

the bottom of my bed. It's against the rules

for her to sleep there, but I guess some rules

can be broken on a birthday—even though,

technically, it's not my *real* birthday yet.

"Is it ok if I sleep late tomorrow?" I ask.

"This was an overwhelming week for all of us.

Grandma Merriday says 'Sundays should be

a day of rest.' Besides, I want to follow

Grandpa Merriday's advice to 'dream big'

about two of my special secrets." Mom nods.

"Do you still feel overwhelmed, Honey?"

"No. I've figured out that feeling

overwhelmed is like catching a cold—like

catching a 'bug.' The feeling disappears, just

like a fever." Mom looks a little sad.

"Are you ok?"

"Very ok, Annabelle, but you're growing so fast that I don't know whether to cheer or cry." *Will I ever understand grown-ups?* "If Andrew sleeps in, too," Mom says, "all of us could rest up for another exciting week. Then, I might have enough brain energy to guess those two special secrets of yours." She gives me her special wink.

Hmmm, maybe I'll share those secrets in Volume Four: <u>My DANGEROUS Week</u>.

~the end~

Sneak Peek: <u>MY DANGEROUS</u> Week

"I told you we shouldn't come here without telling someone!" Kayla whispers. "At least we should have brought your grandma's cell phone!"

"¡Si! ¿Que estaba pensando? —What were you

thinking, Bell?" Carlos demands of me.

"You two weren't so smart when we devised this plan juntos—*together!* And, what if my little brother gets lost, or kidnapped, or hit by a car like Lucky? And what if no one comes in time to save us?"

"Shhhh!" Kayla grabs my arm. "I think I heard a footstep...could be a robber in here!"

"Even if they find us alive, mis padres me van a matar—My parents will kill me!"

"Now just a minute!" I take a deep breath. What did we learn in <u>My OVERWHELMING Week</u>? Stay calm and— *EWWWWWW!* Something's crawling in my hair! On my neck! Something *TERRIBLE!*"

~A~

FUN ACTIVITIES
to turn your memorization
challenges into "sticky" brain solutions!

A. Make up one-word sentences for the

other 8 red states.

B. Use Grandpa Weinstein's secret method

of one-sentence stories to memorize

anything in the world. For example, you

can remember all 50 state capitols in the

U.S.A. Just say the words and listen for

sound-alike tricks. Then repeat your

solutions until they "stick" in your brain.

Try it! Here are three to get you started:

　　1. I DON't knOw why BOYS are
　　NOISEY. = Bois-e, I-dah-o (ID).

2. My PA gave HARRIS a BURGer. = Harrisburg, Pennsylvania (PA) — Annabelle and Andrew's state.

3. He LANded AT The airport to visit his sister GEORGIA. = At-lan-ta, Georgia (GA).

C. You may have fun drawing or writing about something you find overwhelming!

D. With friends, set a timer for three minutes and discover how many things you can list that spin. Examples: a clothes dryer and a dreidel.

E. With an adult, watch the 1956 movie *"The King and I."* Discuss what were the good and bad parts of the story? Was anyone bullied? What lessons did characters learn? Research for the current name of that country.

QUESTIONS to discuss

with a friend, teacher, family member,

or other grown-up:

- How did Carlos know that Annabelle

  has a Havanese puppy?

- What would happen if Carlos

  challenged Daniel to do pirouettes?

- What would you do if you, or a friend,

  were bullied?

- Do you believe that Lucky is a lucky, or

  an unlucky, dog -- or is he both?

  Explain why you feel that way.

- If you could have a pen pal from any

  country, which country would you

  choose? Why?

We hope you will visit:
   www.AnnabellePleaseDontTell.com

For Kids: Find more fun activities, pictures, secrets, adventures, events, audios, videos, gifts, comments and contests.

For Grown-ups: Free educational resources including engaging activities; downloadable-free worksheets/vocabulary lists/thematic concepts & discussion ideas/lesson plans/ composition tools; sharing of parent and educator ideas; author & illustrator contact information.
Information for scheduling an event at your school, library, or community organization.
High-quality, affordable, full-color posters.
Sample:

Thank you! Annabelle-Please-Don't-Tell!

Dear readers, You may use these final pages to sketch, write notes, or exchange autographs with friends.

Made in United States
North Haven, CT
03 September 2022

23622006R00068